Cuatro buenos amigos

Four Good Friends

Los músicos de la ciudad de Bremen/The Bremen Town Musicians
Contado por/Retold by Margaret Hillert
Ilustrado por/Illustrated by Roberta Collier–Morales

NORWOODHOUSE PRESS

Querido padre o tutor: Es posible que los libros de esta serie para lectores principiantes les resulten familiares, ya que las versiones originales de los mismos podrían haber formado parte de sus primeras lecturas. Estos textos, cuidadosamente escritos, incluyen palabras de uso frecuente que le proveen al niño la oportunidad de familiarizarse con las más comúnmente usadas en el lenguaje escrito. Estas nuevas versiones han sido actualizadas y las encantadoras ilustraciones son sumamente atractivas para una nueva generación de pequeños lectores.

Primero, léale el cuento al niño, después permita que él lea las palabras con las que esté familiarizado, y pronto podrá leer solito todo el cuento. En cada paso, elogie el esfuerzo del niño para que desarrolle confianza como lector independiente. Hable sobre las ilustraciones y anime al niño a relacionar el cuento con su propia vida.

Al final del cuento, encontrará actividades relacionadas con la lectura que ayudarán a su niño a practicar y fortalecer sus habilidades como lector. Estas actividades, junto con las preguntas de comprensión, se adhieren a los estándares actuales, de manera que la lectura en casa apoyará directamente los objetivos de instrucción en el salón de clase.

Sobre todo, la parte más importante de toda la experiencia de la lectura es ¡divertirse y disfrutarla!

Dear Caregiver: The books in this Beginning-to-Read collection may look somewhat familiar in that the original versions could have been a part of your own early reading experiences. These carefully written texts feature common sight words to provide your child multiple exposures to the words appearing most frequently in written text. These new versions have been updated and the engaging illustrations are highly appealing to a contemporary audience of young readers.

Begin by reading the story to your child, followed by letting him or her read familiar words and soon your child will be able to read the story independently. At each step of the way, be sure to praise your reader's efforts to build his or her confidence as an independent reader. Discuss the pictures and encourage your child to make connections between the story and his or her own life.

At the end of the story, you will find reading activities that will help your child practice and strengthen beginning reading skills. These activities, along with the comprehension questions are aligned to current standards, so reading efforts at home will directly support the instructional goals in the classroom.

Above all, the most important part of the reading experience is to have fun and enjoy it!

Shannon Cannon

Shannon Cannon, Ph.D., Consultora de lectoescritura / Literacy Consultant

Norwood House Press • www.norwoodhousepress.com
Beginning-to-Read ™ is a registered trademark of Norwood House Press.
Illustration and cover design copyright ©2018 by Norwood House Press. All Rights Reserved.

Authorized Bilingual adaptation from the U.S. English language edition, entitled *Four Good Friends* by Margaret Hillert. Copyright © 2017 Margaret Hillert. Bilingual adaptation Copyright © 2018 Margaret Hillert. Translated and adapted with permission. All rights reserved. Pearson and Cuatro buenos amigos are trademarks, in the US and/or other countries, of Pearson Education, Inc. or its affiliates. This publication is protected by copyright, and prior permission to re-use in any way in any format is required by both Norwood House Press and Pearson Education. This book is authorized in the United States for use in schools and public libraries.

Designer: Ron Jaffe   •   Editorial Production: Lisa Walsh

LIBRARY OF CONGRESS CATALOGING-IN-PUBLICATION DATA

Names: Hillert, Margaret, author. I Collier-Morales, Roberta, illustrator. I
   Del Risco, Eida, translator.
Title: Cuatro buenos amigos = Four good friends / por Margaret Hillert ;
   ilustrado por Roberta Collier-Morales ; traducido por Eida Del Risco.
Other titles: Four good friends I Bremen town musicians. English.
Description: Chicago, Illinois : Norwood House Press, [2017] I Series: A
   beginning-to-read book I Summary: "An easy to read fairy tale about the
   Bremen Town Musicians and their search for a place to live.
   Spanish/English edition includes reading activities"-- Provided by publisher.
Identifiers: LCCN 2016057967 (print) I LCCN 2017014218 (ebook) I ISBN
   9781684040575 (eBook) I ISBN 9781599538433 (library edition : alk. paper)
Subjects: I CYAC: Fairy tales. I Folklore--Germany. I Spanish language materials--Bilingual.
Classification: LCC PZ74 (ebook) I LCC PZ74 .H4438 2017 (print) I DDC 398.2
   [E] --dc23
LC record available at https://lccn.loc.gov/2016057967

Hardcover ISBN: 978-1-59953-843-3   Paperback ISBN: 978-1-68404-042-1

302N—072017
Manufactured in the United States of America in North Mankato, Minnesota.

No puedo trabajar.
Nadie me quiere.
Tengo que irme.
Lejos, lejos, lejos.

I can not work.
No one wants me.
I have to go away.
Away, away, away.

3

Vaya, vaya.
No luces bien, pequeño.
¿Por qué?
¿Qué te pasa?

Oh, my. Oh, my.
You do not look good, little one.
Why?
What is it?

No puedo trabajar.
Nadie me quiere.
No sirvo para nada.

I can not work.
No one wants me.
I am no good.

Ven. Ven.
Me caes bien.
Puedes venir conmigo.

Come. Come.
I like you.
You can come with me.

Presta atención.
Vamos a irnos lejos.
Vamos a encontrar algo.

See here now.
We will go away.
We will find something.

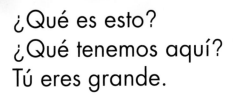

¿Qué es esto?
¿Qué tenemos aquí?
Tú eres grande.

What is this?
What have we here?
You are a big one.

No puedo correr.
No puedo trabajar.
¿Qué voy a hacer ahora?
¿A dónde voy a ir?

I can not run.
I can not work.
What will I do now?
Where will I go?

Eres grande.
Grande, grande, grande.
Nos puedes ayudar.

You are big.
Big, big, big.
You can help us.

Puedes venir con nosotros.
Te queremos.
Ven con nosotros a ver
qué podemos encontrar.

You can come with us.
We want you.
Come with us to see
what we can find.

Caramba, qué bonito eres.
Pero, ¿qué te pasa?
¿Podemos ayudarte?

My, how pretty you are.
But, what is it?
Can we help?

No sirvo para nada,
creo.
Nadie me quiere.
¿Qué puedo hacer?

I am no good,
I guess.
No one wants me.
What am I to do?

¿Quieres venir con nosotros?
Nos caes bien.
Te queremos.

Do you want to come with us?
We like you.
We want you.

Mira ahí.
Una casita.
¿Es eso lo que queremos?

Look here.
A little house.
Is this what we want?

15

Echa una mirada.
¿Qué ves?
¿Qué hay en la casa?

Have a look.
What do you see?
What is in this house?

Veo un hombre.
Veo dos.
Veo tres.

I see a man.
I see two.
I see three.

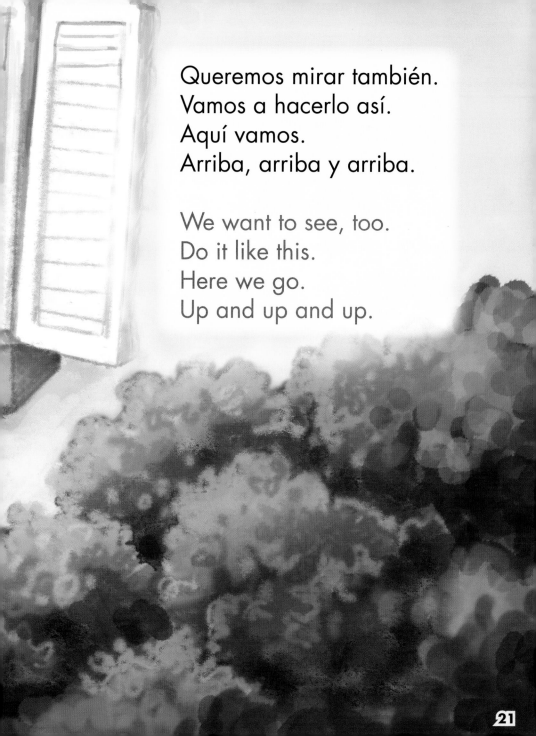

Queremos mirar también.
Vamos a hacerlo así.
Aquí vamos.
Arriba, arriba y arriba.

We want to see, too.
Do it like this.
Here we go.
Up and up and up.

Ay, ay, ay.
Ay, ay. ¡Ay, ay!
¡Ay, miren eso!

Oh, oh, oh!
Oh, my. Oh, my!
Oh, look at that!

¡Fuera de aquí! ¡Fuera de aquí!
No es bueno que estemos aquí.
¡Huyamos! ¡Huyamos!
Corran, corran, corran.

Get out! Get out!
It is not good for us here.
Get away! Get away!
Run, run, run.

Esto es gracioso.
¿Qué hicimos?
Pero vamos a entrar.
Aquí dentro se está bien.

Now that is funny.
What did we do?
But come in here.
It looks good in here.

Ahora tenemos una casa.
Tenemos algo que comer.
No podemos trabajar.
Pero somos felices.

Now we have a house.
We have something to eat.
We can not work.
But we are happy.

Foundational Skills

In addition to reading the numerous high-frequency words in the text, this book also supports the development of foundational skills.

Phonological Awareness: The /f/ sound

Oral Blending: Say the beginning sounds listed below and ask your child to say the word formed by adding the /**f**/ sound to the end:

roo + /f/ = roof	lea + /f/ = leaf	che + /f/ = chef
hu + /f/ = huff	li + /f/ = life	wol + /f/ = wolf
loa + /f/ = loaf	bee + /f/ = beef	el + /f/ = elf
shel + /f/ = shelf	kni + /f/ = knife	scar + /f/ = scarf

Phonics: The letter Ff

1. Demonstrate how to form the letters **F** and **f** for your child.
2. Have your child practice writing **F** and **f** at least three times each.
3. Ask your child to point to the words in the book that begin with the letter **f**.
4. Write down the following words and ask your child to circle the letter **f** in each word:

for	fun	raft	fur	foot
fast	roof	if	sift	friend
fold	lift	fluff	flat	stuff

Fluency: Shared Reading

1. Reread the story to your child at least two more times while your child tracks the print by running a finger under the words as they are read. Ask your child to read the words he or she knows with you.
2. Reread the story taking turns, alternating readers between sentences or pages.

Language

The concepts, illustrations, and text help children develop language both explicitly and implicitly.

Vocabulary: Synonyms

1. Write the following words on separate pieces of paper:

small	scared	house	thin	joyful
big	slender	nice	happy	afraid
little	excellent	tired	run	make
sleepy	jog	large	create	pretty
good	home	lovely	great	

2. Read each word to your child and ask your child to repeat it.
3. Explain to your child that when two different words mean almost the same thing, they are called synonyms.
4. Mix the words up. Point to a word and ask your child to read it. Provide clues if your child needs them. Ask your child to match the pairs of synonym words.

Reading Literature and Informational Text

To support comprehension, ask your child the following questions. The answers either come directly from the text or require inferences and discussion.

Key Ideas and Detail

- Ask your child to retell the sequence of events in the story.
- What did the four friends have in common?

Craft and Structure

- Is this a book that tells a story or one that gives information? How do you know?
- How did the animals help each other?

Integration of Knowledge and Ideas

- Why do you think the men left the house?
- Can you describe a time when you felt bad but everything turned out okay?

Margaret Hillert ha ayudado a millones de niños de todo el mundo a aprender a leer independientemente. Fue maestra de primer grado por 34 años y durante esa época empezó a escribir libros con los que sus estudiantes pudieran ganar confianza en la lectura y pudieran, al mismo tiempo, disfrutarla. Ha escrito más de 100 libros para niños que comienzan a leer. De niña, disfrutaba escribiendo poesía y, de adulta, continuó su escritura poética tanto para niños como para adultos.

Photograph by Glenna Washburn

Margaret Hillert has helped millions of children all over the world learn to read independently. She was a first grade teacher for 34 years and during that time started writing books that her students could both gain confidence in reading and enjoy. She wrote well over 100 books for children just learning to read. As a child, she enjoyed writing poetry and continued her poetic writings as an adult for both children and adults.

Roberta Collier-Morales ha ilustrado libros para niños y materiales educativos, comerciales y religiosos por más de 33 años. Ha creado arte para telas e impresiones artísticas. Trabaja en un estudio con vista a las montañas de Colorado, con dos perros, dos gatos, tres pececitos, su hijo y su mamá. www.robertacolliermorales.com

Roberta Collier-Morales has been illustrating children's books, educational materials, mass market, and religious subjects for over 33 years. She creates art for fabric and fine art prints. She works in a studio with a view of the mountains in Colorado with her two dogs, two cats, three goldfish, son and mom. www.robertacolliermorales.com